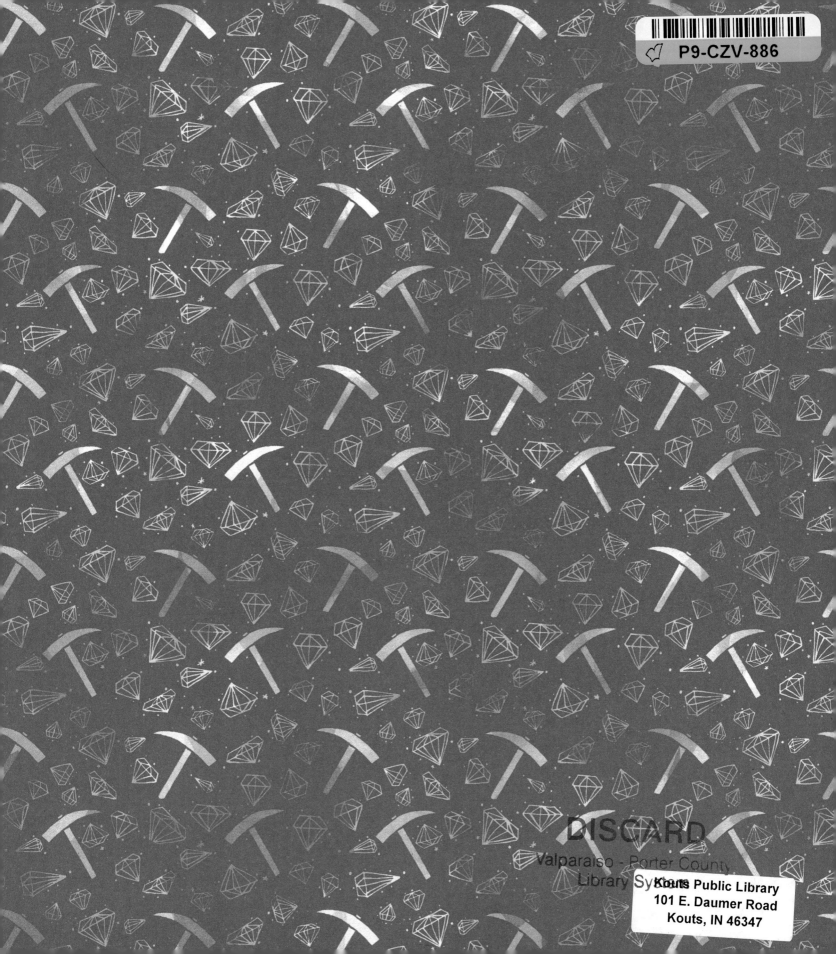

SNOW WHITE and the 77 DWARFS

davide cali

raphaëlle barbanègre

TUNDRA BOOKS

ONCE UPON A TIME, somewhere
deep in the woods, a girl named
Snow White was running away from a
terrible witch. She came across a tiny
house that belonged to 77 dwarfs.

The dwarfs were very kind. They said
Snow White could stay with them if she
would help with their chores.

Snow White could see right away that life with the dwarfs might be difficult. For starters, how was she going to learn all their names?

And there was **A LOT** to do.

First came the laundry.

Then there was beard maintenance.

After that, every dwarf
wanted a bedtime story.
His **OWN** bedtime story.

Early the next morning,
everyone was ready
for breakfast—all
at the same time,
OF COURSE!

THEN there were 77 little lunches to pack,
with a sandwich and a juice box in each.

Before Snow White could even BLINK, it was time for dinner!

After all that, she still had the dishes to wash.

Yes, the dwarfs were kind. But they were also messy, rambunctious, naughty and VERY, VERY LOUD.

THE PLACE WAS A ZOO!

It was all **TOO MUCH** for Snow White! She decided to leave and take her chances with the witch.

Now, somewhere deep in the
woods, a girl named Snow White
is sleeping, waiting to be woken
by a kiss . . .

. . . oh, no, she's **NOT**!

PLEASE
DON'T
WAKE ME UP

thank you

To Clément, who kept me from going nuts
drawing 77 dwarfs—R.B.

Text copyright © 2015 by Davide Cali
Illustrations copyright © 2015 by Raphaëlle Barbanègre

Published in Canada by Tundra Books, a division of Random House of
Canada Limited, One Toronto Street, Suite 300, Toronto, Ontario M5C 2V6

Published in the United States by Tundra Books of Northern New York,
P.O. Box 1030, Plattsburgh, New York 12901

Library of Congress Control Number: 2014941838

Library and Archives Canada Cataloguing in Publication

Calì, Davide, 1972–, author
    Snow White and the seventy-seven dwarfs / Davide Cali ;
illustrated by Raphaëlle Barbanègre.

Issued in print and electronic formats.
ISBN 978-1-77049-763-4 (bound).—ISBN 978-1-77049-765-8 (epub)

    1. Snow White (Tale)—Adaptations. I. Barbanègre, Raphaëlle, 1985–, illustrator II. Title.

PZ7.C1283Sn 2015   j823'.92   C2014-903063-0
                                                                C2014-903064-9

Edited by Samantha Swenson
Designed by Five Seventeen
The text was set in Arrus, Anarko, and Folk.

www.tundrabooks.com

Printed and bound in China

1 2 3 4 5 6   20 19 18 17 16 15

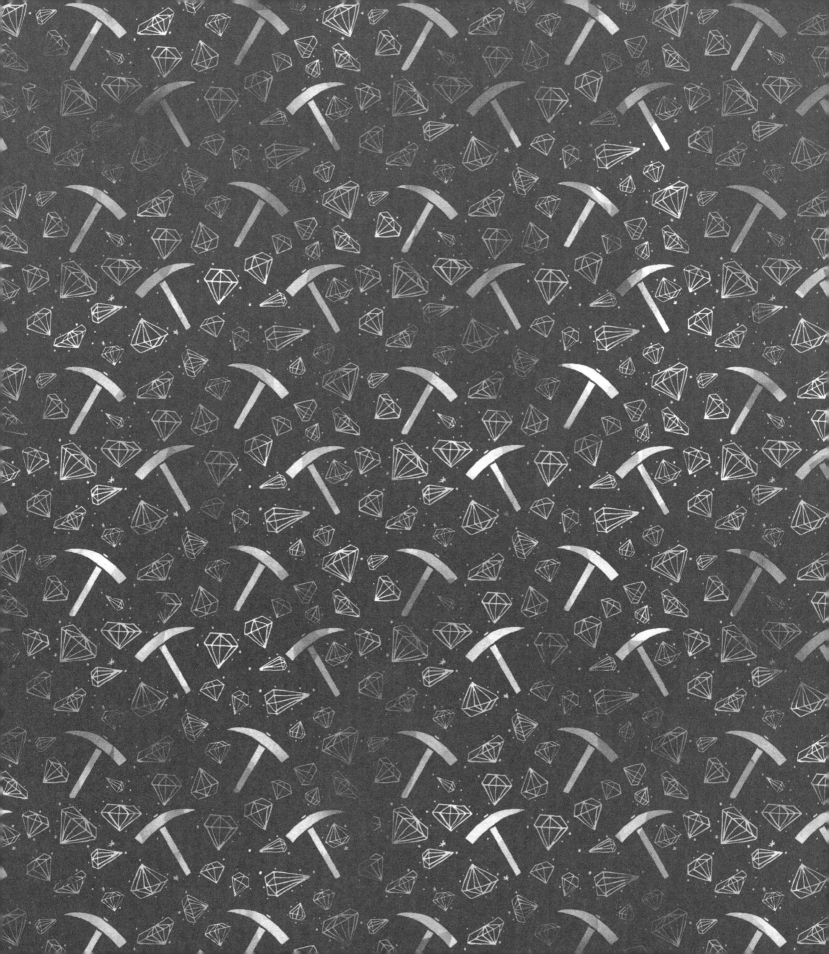